Flight
of the Last Dragon

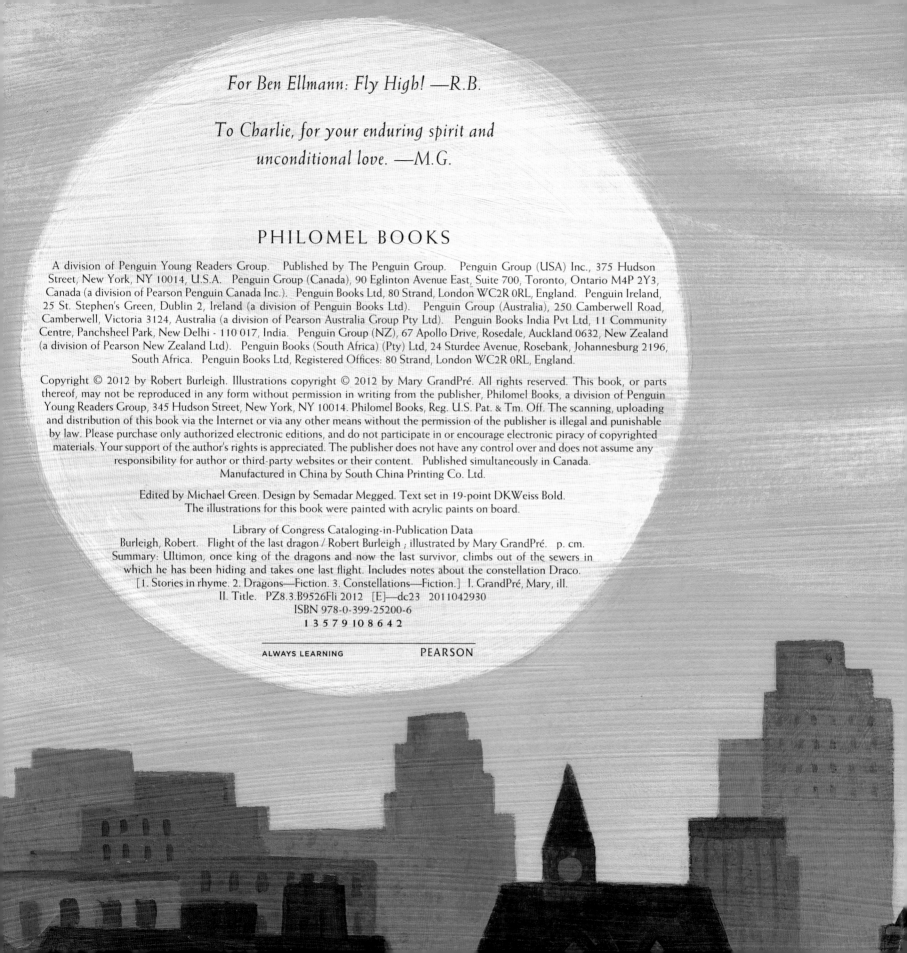

For Ben Ellmann: Fly High! —R.B.

To Charlie, for your enduring spirit and
unconditional love. —M.G.

PHILOMEL BOOKS

A division of Penguin Young Readers Group.   Published by The Penguin Group.   Penguin Group (USA) Inc., 375 Hudson Street, New York, NY 10014, U.S.A.   Penguin Group (Canada), 90 Eglinton Avenue East, Suite 700, Toronto, Ontario M4P 2Y3, Canada (a division of Pearson Penguin Canada Inc.).   Penguin Books Ltd, 80 Strand, London WC2R 0RL, England.   Penguin Ireland, 25 St. Stephen's Green, Dublin 2, Ireland (a division of Penguin Books Ltd).   Penguin Group (Australia), 250 Camberwell Road, Camberwell, Victoria 3124, Australia (a division of Pearson Australia Group Pty Ltd).   Penguin Books India Pvt Ltd, 11 Community Centre, Panchsheel Park, New Delhi - 110 017, India.   Penguin Group (NZ), 67 Apollo Drive, Rosedale, Auckland 0632, New Zealand (a division of Pearson New Zealand Ltd).   Penguin Books (South Africa) (Pty) Ltd, 24 Sturdee Avenue, Rosebank, Johannesburg 2196, South Africa.   Penguin Books Ltd, Registered Offices: 80 Strand, London WC2R 0RL, England.

Edited by Michael Green. Design by Semadar Megged. Text set in 19-point DKWeiss Bold.
The illustrations for this book were painted with acrylic paints on board.

Library of Congress Cataloging-in-Publication Data
Burleigh, Robert. Flight of the last dragon / Robert Burleigh ; illustrated by Mary GrandPré.   p. cm.
Summary: Ultimon, once king of the dragons and now the last survivor, climbs out of the sewers in which he has been hiding and takes one last flight. Includes notes about the constellation Draco.
[1. Stories in rhyme. 2. Dragons—Fiction. 3. Constellations—Fiction.] I. GrandPré, Mary, ill.
II. Title.   PZ8.3.B9526Fli 2012   [E]—dc23   2011042930
ISBN 978-0-399-25200-6
1 3 5 7 9 10 8 6 4 2

Flight
of the
Last Dragon

ROBERT BURLEIGH   MARY GRANDPRÉ

PHILOMEL BOOKS   An Imprint of Penguin Group (USA) Inc.

Come, if you dare,
Deep underground.
Make no whisper.
Shhh! No sound.

Below the city.
Far from the sun!
Beneath the subway,
Where sewers run!

Where mice squeak,
And rats mumble,
And distant train wheels
Rattle and rumble.

For here is his home!
Oh, gaze upon
The last of the dragons—

Ultimon!

Poor Ultimon,
Once a king,
Now shivers and shakes,
A pitiful thing.

His scales are rusted,
His feathers are splattered,
His talons are dulled,
His wings are tattered.

Weak, alone,
He wades in the slime,
Lost in dreams
Of a long-ago time.

A time when dragons
Ruled the waves
And breathed hot flames
In jewel-filled caves.

Hot tears rain down!
Sobs Ultimon:
"I knew them all!
Now all are gone!

And I am left
With thoughts that pass
Like grains of sand
In an hourglass."

But shhh. Listen.
Traffic slows.
The subway sleeps.
The daylight goes.

Up through his manhole,
See Ultimon rise
As tall buildings blink
Like dragon eyes.

He beats on the wall
Of the chill night sky.
He breathes. Flames sputter.
He utters a cry.

"Please, please, someone—
Have pity on
A dragon king
Called Ultimon!"

At first his cry
Fades into black.
But then a small voice
Answers back.

Deep in the night,
A single star
Seems to call out,
You must go far.

There is a place—
Lift up! Fly!
Ultimon, Ultimon.
Into the sky.

He raises his head.
He turns to listen.
His tail quivers.
His eyes glisten.

But can he fly?
He stumbles and blinks.
His wings droop.
His heart sinks.

Once more the voice,
First faint, and then,
Louder and louder:
Try. Try again.

He shudders, he stands.
With all his might,
He gathers strength
For his final flight.

He pushes off.
He flings back his mane.
He feels wind rush
As his muscles strain.

Aha! He's up!
The sweep! The glide!
Talons thrust out,
Wings flung wide!

A late-night worker
On the 90th floor
Spies a blur—
And nothing more.

A child turning
In her bed
Hears feathers whirring
Overhead.

A lonely stroller
Through a park
Sees a green glow
Light the dark.

A beautiful something—
So high and far—
A dragon-colored
Shooting star!

Farther and farther,
He travels on,
Drawn by a voice:
Come, Ultimon!

Onward and upward!
Cold and alone!
Through clouds of dust,
Past moons of stone.

His body aches
At every turn.
Ice coats his feathers.
His hot lungs burn.

One star he sights—
A twinkling jewel
Reflected in
The sky's dark pool.

Closer, closer,
Our dragon flies.
Until pure starlight
Blinds his eyes.

And he seems to sense
Friends all around,
Sparkling gently
Without a sound.

Come in, Ultimon,
Out of the night!
Come in, Ultimon,
Into the light!

Now scales are golden,
Now feathers are glowing,
Now talons glitter,
Now wings are flowing.

Home at last.
His journey won,
His great flight over,
His work is done.

Walk out, reader,
In the blackest night—
Gaze up where the stars
Are crisp and bright.

Next to the polestar
That guides with its beams—
See! A dragon
Constellation gleams.

Can you find Draco,
The dragon star?
Ultimon, Ultimon,
There you are!

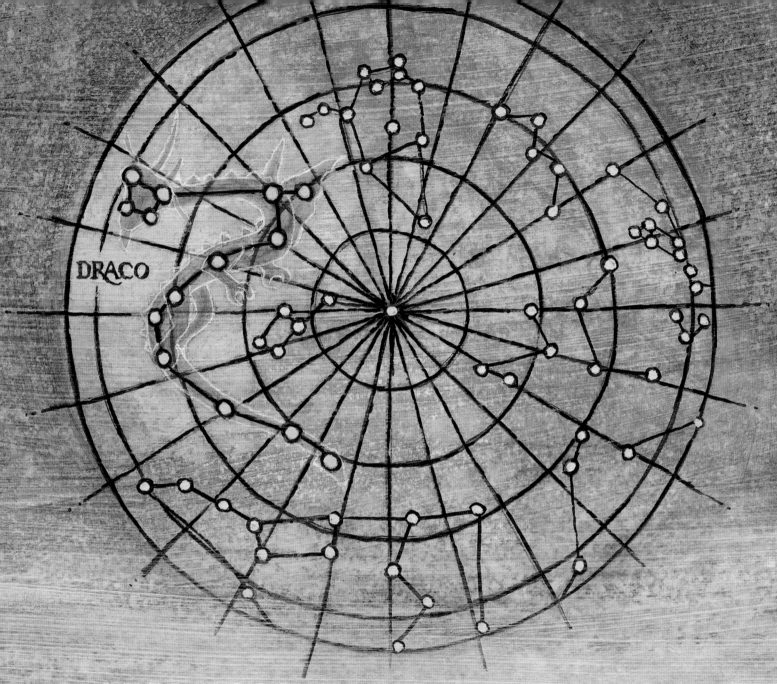

DRACO

AFTERWORD Dragons may (or may not) be real. But Draco the Dragon is real! It's a constellation that shines in our northern skies. In fact, it's very near the North Star, which always points the way north.

The constellation got its name long ago. It contains many stars that—if you look up on a clear night—seem to trace the outline of a dragon's head and body. Getting a book on constellations will help you. The square-shaped head consists of four stars, and the body winds around and ends in a long dragon tail.

Look for it—and remember Ultimon!